WOMBAT, MUDLARK

& OTHER STORIES

for my mother and grandmother,
who filled my life with stories

WOMBAT, MUDLARK

& OTHER STORIES

Helen Milroy

 FREMANTLE PRESS

CONTENTS

WOMBAT

&

MOTHER

EARTH

Some children are just like the wombat in this story. They are the dreamers who inspire us with their imagination and wonder. They are exceptional children and wise beyond their years.

Since the beginning of time, Mother Earth had looked after everything and everyone, asking for nothing in return. Mother Earth had helped the trees to grow, the flowers to bloom, the animals to live and the rivers to run. But now that everything was thriving, everyone forgot about Mother Earth. Mother Earth was sad and lonely. She felt empty and cold. Although the sun came up every day to warm Mother Earth, by sunset the warmth had already left her like a willy-willy disappearing into the sky. One night, Mother Earth was so cold she started to cry. Wombat was fast asleep under a tree and woke abruptly from his dreaming.

'What is going on?' he asked. 'Who is that crying?'

'It is me,' said Mother Earth. 'I am sorry I woke you but I am so cold and sad, I can't stop shivering. I don't know what has happened to me but I haven't felt happy for a very long time. I don't know what to do,' she sobbed.

'Oh dear,' said Wombat, 'let me see if I can help you.'

Wombat felt very sorry for Mother

Earth. He had never seen her like this before. Wombat loved Mother Earth and all the wonderful things she had helped to create. So Wombat started to tell Mother Earth of the many beautiful discoveries he made each day and of the wondrous dreams he had every night. He told her how much he loved and cherished her.

'None of us would survive without you,' said Wombat.

Wombat and Mother Earth talked and laughed together until the early hours of the morning. Wombat was so pleased to have someone to share his stories with, and Mother Earth loved hearing them.

'I am no longer feeling so cold,' said Mother Earth. 'For the first time in a long time, I feel warm and happy.'

'That may be so,' said Wombat, 'but now I am freezing after sitting up most of the night!'

'Dig a deep burrow into the soft earth and I will keep you warm and safe in my belly until the sun wakes up for the day,' said Mother Earth.

Up until that night, Wombat had always slept on top of the ground. Each night he tried to find some soft leaves or a warm place to sleep. Sometimes it took ages for Wombat to find the right spot and this shortened his dreamtime. Sometimes when the sun woke him up in the morning, he hadn't finished his dreaming and would wake very grumpy. Wombat was excited at the idea of sleeping in the belly of Mother Earth, it would be warm and cosy. Even the pesky sun wouldn't be able to wake him up and he could dream as much as he liked.

'That is a great idea,' said Wombat, who was now exhausted and desperate to return to his dreamtime. Wombat dug the burrow deep into Mother Earth and fell into a strange sleep. Each breath Wombat took tickled Mother Earth's belly and Mother Earth giggled, but when Wombat snored, Mother Earth laughed out loud. Mother Earth was feeling warm and content looking after Wombat, while Wombat felt snug and safe in his burrow. Soon Wombat started to dream and something magical happened. The power and wonder of Wombat's dreams swirled around Mother Earth's belly and filled her with love, joy and hope. Mother Earth could now see clearly once again and realised what was wrong.

At the beginning of time, Mother Earth was born with an eternal flame buried deep in her heart underground. The flame had started to falter and her heart was struggling. Mother Earth was exhausted from always looking after everyone else. Now she needed someone to look after her.

The love and wonder from Wombat's dreams were exactly what Mother Earth needed. They surged like electricity along invisible threads that wove through the earth, awakening the eternal flame and creating a furnace that warmed her completely. Mother Earth's heart started to glow and its beat grew stronger and stronger, setting in motion rivers of light that radiated throughout Mother Earth. It was like the dawning of the first day, when hope broke through the darkness and the future became possible.

Through Wombat's dream, Mother Earth was able to see all of what she had helped to create and how much love there was in the world.

Mother Earth was so grateful, she made sure Wombat was safe and sound until he awoke to start the new day full of stories yet to be told. Mother Earth even kept the sun from shining into the burrow until Wombat had finished his dreamtime.

In the morning Wombat woke feeling refreshed like never before.

'That was the best dreaming I have ever done,' said Wombat. 'I am going to sleep in my burrow every night from now on! I am also going to make sure everyone looks after you as they should!'

'That would be wonderful,' said Mother Earth. 'I promise to watch over you every night so you can dream your dreams for everyone!'

Mother Earth never felt cold and sad again, and Wombat never again woke up grumpy. Mother Earth and Wombat loved sharing the stories and dreams together.

Every night, Wombat crawled into his burrow ready to begin his dreaming.

Every night, Mother Earth watched and waited for the dreaming to begin.

MUDLARK

&

SUN

Some children are just like the mudlark in this story. They have a strong emotional intelligence and will share the joys and burdens in life. They are extraordinary children and unwavering in their support for others.

When Mudlark was a little fluffy chick just out of the nest, she loved rolling in mud and playing in the mud-pool. Sometimes she would play all day but by late afternoon, the mud pool would be cold. Mudlark would shiver and her beak would make a funny chattering noise.

'What is that strange sound?' said Sun one day.

'It's me,' said Mudlark. 'I'm freezing.'

Sun looked down, but all he saw was a ball of mud.

Mudlark wiped the mud off her face. 'See,' she said.

Sun laughed at the little bird. 'I will warm you up,' he said, and he did. From then on Mudlark and Sun became good friends.

One day Sun started to become angry. He woke up angry, he went to bed angry and he was fiery all day long. Sun's anger increased day after day. Soon Sun was so angry he hardly set at all. The animals were getting tired because there was too much light and heat to sleep. They were worried that one day Sun might set the land on fire. They didn't know what to do. The water was disappearing and even Mudlark's favourite mud pool was turning to dust. Something had to be done. The days had become so hot, the animals had started living underground.

Mudlark knew Sun hadn't always been like this. Sun used to be the best sun in the universe. Something must have happened, thought Mudlark.

'It can't be very nice for anyone to be feeling that way all the time,' said Mudlark to all the animals. 'Perhaps I should try and talk to him.'

'You do that,' said the animals. 'We are fed up and want Sun to go away.'

'Sun,' Mudlark called out. 'Sun!'

Sun wasn't listening. Solar flares kept

firing off all over the sky, sometimes leaving hot burning coals to fall to the ground. Mudlark threw mud-pies at Sun to get his attention but as soon as they got close, they were burnt into dust and blew away.

Mudlark decided she needed help. That night, she went to talk to Sun's oldest friend, Moon.

'Do you know why Sun is so angry?' Mudlark asked Moon.

'Well, he has always had a hot temper, you know,' said Moon, 'but I don't know what is wrong with him. He keeps making me wait later and later to rise in the evening and then he gets up very early. Sun was always determined, but he never used to be this angry. Perhaps you should ask his cousin, Comet. Comet visited Sun not so long ago. Maybe Comet knows what is wrong.'

'Thank you,' said Mudlark, 'but how am I to find Comet?' Comet only visited the earth every few years. Mudlark had no idea where he would be now.

'I could ask the stars,' said Moon. 'They stretch for miles and are always gossiping about what is going on across the universe, so they might know where he is.'

The stars sent a message out through the constellations and soon everyone was chattering about Comet.

It didn't take long for Comet to hear

what was happening. Comet quickly turned around to pay Mudlark a visit.

Mudlark woke with a startle to a bright light hovering overhead. Mudlark and Comet talked for ages. Comet had known Sun since the beginning of time. Comet told Mudlark that when the universe was created there were so many children of the sun parents, there was little time for play. The little earth sun was always worried and had trouble settling to sleep. Everybody was concerned he would burn up the whole universe. His grandmother, however, adored him and would often tell him stories and play games to teach him how to be a good earth sun. She even wrote him a special lullaby which she sang every night to help him settle and create the most beautiful sunsets before going to bed. He really loved his grandmother.

'When I visited recently,' said Comet, 'I had to tell Sun some sad news. His grandmother had set for the last time. He was heartbroken.'

'Now I understand,' said Mudlark. 'Can you teach me the lullaby?' she asked.

Mudlark and Comet practiced the lullaby all night until she sang it just right. The next day was so hot no one could go outside at all, so Mudlark rested until late in the afternoon. Then Mudlark gathered up her last bit of water to make some mud and covered herself with a thick coating.

Sun was at the edge of the earth but

was refusing to set. Mudlark flew towards Sun, covered in her mud coat so she could get as close to Sun as possible without getting burnt. Mudlark started singing the lullaby as loudly as she could. Sun stopped immediately when he heard the song and just listened. The fiery flames started to dissipate and the harsh light softened. The temperature started falling and suddenly rainclouds rolled across the sky. Rain poured out all over the land, filling the rivers and lakes and the mud pools. All the animals came out to see what was happening. Mudlark stood fast and kept singing. As the storm passed over, Mudlark was finishing the last verse of the song.

All the mud had washed off Mudlark

and her feathers glistened with raindrops. Sun looked down.

'It was you singing, Mudlark,' said Sun with great joy.

'Yes,' said Mudlark. 'Comet taught me your lullaby. I am so sorry about your grandmother.' 'I was trying to be strong and hide my grief,' said Sun, 'but I didn't realise what I was doing. The rain was my tears for my grandmother.'

'It's okay,' said Mudlark. 'We don't always understand or know what to do with our feelings, but you can always talk to me, Sun.'

Mudlark was still dripping wet and getting a bit cold. Sun shone just a little brighter to warm her up, then cast a beautiful rainbow overhead. It was the most magnificent sunset the world had ever seen. All the animals were overjoyed to see Sun back to his usual self.

From then on, every evening and whenever Sun requested it, Mudlark would sing him his grandmother's lullaby. In return, Sun warmed the mud pool for Mudlark every afternoon so she could play happily all day.

DINGO
&
MOON

Some children are just like the dingo in this story. They are the eternal optimists and will always bring light and hope to dark places. They are wonderful children and are kind and helpful to others.

A long time ago when the earth was formed, it was in complete darkness. All of the animals were in a deep sleep waiting for the dawning of the first day. When the earth sun was ready, he travelled a long way to take his place in the sky. As Sun neared the earth, morning appeared with a gentle light spreading across the landscape, waking all of the animals from their dreamtime. The animals saw their country for the first time and it was magnificent.

With great excitement, the animals explored the landscape and saw the forests, mountains and rivers. At the end of the first day, Sun was tired and wanted to go to sleep. Sun warned the animals that his light would soon fade and would not return until the morning. All the animals scurried back to their homes for fear of getting lost in the dark. As Sun set, the earth once again fell into complete darkness. On the second day, the animals asked Sun if he could keep some light in the sky during the night, but Sun said he needed his sleep, otherwise he would not be able to warm the day and help the earth to grow. The animals tried to make sure no one was ever left alone in the darkness.

Meanwhile, far away in the outer heavens, all the moons were getting ready to take their place in the universe. The earth moon was very shy and nervous. When it was time for her to travel to earth, she panicked and lost her way. Moon found herself in a distant dark galaxy all alone. Moon was scared and started to cry. It was so cold that her tears turned into ice crystals. The ice quickly surrounded Moon, trapping her. The more she sobbed, the thicker the ice wall became. No one could hear Moon's cries.

Back on earth, the animals loved their days roaming around country but still feared the darkness at nighttime. In the forest lived a large family of dingoes with lots of pups. One little dingo loved visiting and playing with all the animals and often travelled far from home chasing geckoes. Everyone loved Little Dingo, even the geckoes. Little Dingo knew where everyone lived and was always helping gather the little ones and get them safely back to their homes before dark.

One day Little Dingo was helping a baby wombat return to his den at sunset. Wombat was too heavy for Little Dingo to carry and Wombat walked so slowly that it took ages to reach his family. This left Little Dingo too far away from his own home when the darkness came. As the light faded, Little Dingo desperately tried to run home. Poor Little Dingo, he just could not find his way in the dark and could not even see where to shelter for the long night ahead. Little Dingo ran around frantically but he kept tripping over and bumping into things. He ended up falling into a deep crevice in the mountain. Little Dingo knew no one would be able to come looking for him until the morning. He was so scared he started to howl. He howled and howled and howled long into the night. His call echoed through the mountains and was amplified across the universe. His cry pierced the outer heavens and shattered the ice wall of tears holding Moon. Moon was finally free.

Moon could hear Little Dingo's howl

and she knew in her heart she had to follow his voice. She no longer had to find her way across the universe on her own, she had Little Dingo guiding her to her rightful place above the earth. The shattered ice crystals slowly fell across the darkness to form stars along the path left by Moon in her hurried escape. As Moon arrived at the earth, a gentle glow surrounded Little Dingo. Little Dingo looked up in surprise to see a beautiful new moon smiling down at him, shrouded in a glittering night sky.

'You found me and rescued me,' said Moon gratefully.

'And you found me and rescued me!' said Little Dingo with great relief.

Moon gently laid down some moon dust to help Little Dingo climb out of the crevice and gave him a moonbeam to help him light the path on his way home.

All of the animals were overjoyed with Little Dingo's return and praised him for bringing light into the darkness. In celebration, all the dingoes got together that night and sang a welcome song to Moon and her stars.

Every evening Little Dingo would sing to Moon so she never felt scared or alone again. And every night Moon would light Little Dingo's path so he could always find his way home in the darkness — but Dingo kept his moonbeam close by just in case.

PENGUIN
&
SKY

Some children are just like the penguin in this story. They seem to know about family and where everyone belongs. They are remarkable children and make for loyal and faithful friends.

P enguin was a very clever fellow.
In particular, Penguin was a brilliant
navigator. He could journey across both
land and sea. He knew where everything
was in Sky, and that is how he found his
way around. Penguin understood where
everyone belonged and was always able to
find anyone who was lost.

One morning Penguin looked up at
Sky and noticed emptiness was showing

through in big patches. Everything had moved about and Penguin felt confused.

'Sky, why are you losing your colour?' asked Penguin. 'And why is everything in the wrong places?'

'I am worried,' Sky confided to Penguin, 'I don't know what is happening and it seems to be getting worse. If it keeps spreading, we will all disappear into the emptiness!'

'This is serious,' said Penguin.

Penguin set off to look for the blue by following where the emptiness was at its strongest. He climbed up to the top of a huge iceberg and looked out to sea. Suddenly, he heard a big splash and looked around to see an enormous whale leaping into Sky. Each time the whale came out of the water it spun around and wrapped itself in Sky, taking with it some of the blue.

'Whale,' Penguin called out, 'what are you doing?'

Whale was startled and hid under the water. Penguin waited and waited for Whale to re-surface. Finally, Whale lay on his side close to the water's edge so he could see if Penguin was still there.

'I can see you, Whale,' said Penguin. 'Don't be scared, come and talk to me and I will help you.'

Whale came up alongside Penguin. He was the strangest looking whale Penguin had ever seen. He had blotches of blue all over his large grey body.

Whale began to tell Penguin his story.
Whale had been alone for a very long
time. When he was a young whale, he
had often gotten lost because he went off
exploring on his own. He would miss the
big whale journeys across the seas and his
family would have to go searching for him.
One day however, he ventured too far and
was lost completely. Ever since, he had
been searching the oceans for his family.
The big grey whales had disappeared and
Whale thought he was the only one left.
He had almost given up all hope when he
had an idea.

'I haven't been able to find my own
family,' Whale explained to Penguin. 'I

thought if I turned myself into a blue whale instead, I might be able to have a new family. I have seen some blue whales swimming past and I thought I could join them.'

Penguin felt so sorry for Whale. 'I will help you find your family,' said Penguin, 'but you must stop taking the blue from Sky. Look up, Whale. The holes in Sky are getting bigger and soon the emptiness will take over and we will all be lost forever!'

'I am so sorry,' said Whale, 'I didn't realise I was destroying Sky. I thought there was so much blue that Sky wouldn't notice.' Whale started to cry.

'It's all right, Whale. I understand. But

we will have to find a way to put the blue back,' said Penguin. 'If I am going to find your family, all the things in Sky must be in their rightful place.'

'I have an idea,' said Whale.

Whale told Penguin what to do. Penguin climbed onto Whale's back and started scraping the blue off his skin. Penguin put the blue carefully into the breathing hole on top of Whale's head.

'Let's see if this works,' said Whale. 'Stand back, Penguin!'

Whale took a big gulp of water and a deep breath. With all his might he blew the blue out of the blowhole up into Sky.

'Wow,' said Penguin, 'that was amazing!' They continued painting Sky until all the emptiness was gone. Sky looked beautiful and everything returned to its rightful place.

Sky was so relieved and happy. 'I am glad everything is back to normal,' Sky said with a big sigh.

'Not quite,' said Penguin. 'Now we have to find Whale a family.'

'I can swim long distances and am quite fast,' said Whale. 'I can help.

'Of course you can. We will find them together. We are family now too, you know!' said Penguin.

'I seem to remember watching a small grey whale swimming around in the Southern Ocean just a few days ago,' said Sky.

'Let's hurry,' said Whale, getting quite excited.

'Now everything is back in its place, I can easily navigate our way across the ocean,' said Penguin.

Penguin and Whale set off across the ocean as fast as they could, but they had a long way to go.

Whale started singing his beautiful whale song full of hope and love. Sky had an idea. He sent a gentle breeze to cradle the whale song and lift it up into the heavens. The fastest winds of all lived up there and they agreed to carry the song ahead of Penguin and Whale. This was much faster than leaving the song to travel through the water.

Sure enough, there was a small grey whale gently lolling about in the Southern Ocean. Small Grey Whale had been feeding and was preparing to swim the long voyage north. She was just about to set off when Sky sent the breeze down from the heavens to swirl around her.

She stopped and looked around. She couldn't believe what she was hearing! She, too, had thought she was the only whale left. She was almost too scared to hope there was another.

'Maybe I am dreaming,' she thought to herself. She dived deep into the water but when she surfaced she could still hear the song.

'It must be real,' she thought. She

frantically searched nearby but could not find another whale.

She was just about to give up hope when she felt the vibrations of the whale song through the water. She looked up and saw the strangest sight. A penguin was sailing across the water at great speed on the back of a big grey whale! Over the next few days there was great rejoicing and celebration.

'I will never stray again,' said Whale.

'No, you won't, because you will have me by your side,' said Small Grey Whale.

'And if you do,' said Penguin, 'you will always have me and Sky to find you.'

BROLGA
&
LITTLE STAR

Some children are like the brolga in
this story. They have a great energy
and enthusiasm for life.
They are inspirational children, always
encouraging others to embrace what
life has to offer.

Brolga was a very energetic bird. She was always running around and getting into trouble.

'Please stop fidgeting,' said the other birds. 'You are so clumsy, you are driving us crazy!' Brolga was upset. She just wanted to help but she always seemed to get in the way. Brolga decided to go for a long walk. She was skipping and hopping and jumping along the path when she came across a fallen star. The star was losing its sparkle and turning grey.

'What is the matter, Little Star?' Brolga asked.

'I have fallen from the sky and I am not sure how to find my way home again. I can't stay on earth for too long. I need the heavens to renew my sparkle otherwise I will turn to stone,' said Little Star.

'That is very bad luck,' said Brolga. 'Perhaps you can come and live with me and I will look after you until we can find your way home.'

'Oh, thank you,' said Little Star. So off they set, back to Brolga's nest.

Little Star watched Brolga for some time. Brolga was always moving about and

didn't always seem to know what to do
with all her energy.

'Have you thought about dancing?'
Little Star asked Brolga.

'Me? Dance?' Brolga giggled. 'Dancing
is for the graceful birds. I am too clumsy
for dancing.'

Little Star felt sorry for Brolga. Brolga
was kind and strong, full of life and always
trying to help others, but she wasn't happy.

'Well, Brolga,' said Little Star, 'just try
swaying in time with my sparkles.'

Little Star started sparkling very slowly
and Brolga stretched out her lovely wings
and swayed back and forth.

'Now, try tapping your feet,' said Little
Star, as she started to sparkle a little faster.

Brolga tapped her feet and waved her wings.

'This is great fun,' said Brolga, as she added in turns and leaps and swirling motions to her movements.

Little Star started clapping. 'Bravo, bravo, Brolga, you are a wonderful dancer.'

Brolga took a deep bow and laughed to herself. Maybe I can dance after all, she thought.

'Thank you so much for teaching me, Little Star,' said Brolga. 'Tomorrow we will start looking for your way home.'

Every morning Brolga and Little Star went searching for a way into the sky, and every night they danced and danced. But as time passed, Little Star became

homesick and her sparkles faded more
and more. Soon she would be too weak to
sparkle at all. Brolga was worried for her
friend.

'Do you think we will ever find my way
home?' asked Little Star.

'I am sure we will,' answered Brolga.
'We just need to stay strong.'

Now the other birds had been watching
Brolga and Little Star come and go
each day and had grown curious. In the
evening, they could hear Brolga and Little
Star laughing and jumping about.

Brolga and Little Star always seemed
to be having so much fun, the other birds
were jealous.

'What are you and Little Star up to?'

asked the other birds.

'Why don't you come and see for yourself,' said Brolga. 'Meet us down on the mud flats tomorrow night and we will show you.'

As the sun set, all the birds gathered together to wait for Brolga and Little Star.

'What is taking so long? Where are they?' the birds muttered amongst themselves.

Suddenly they all went quiet as they could see a light sparkling in the distance. Even though Little Star was getting weaker and weaker, she used all of her strength to help Brolga dance. Brolga appeared and began walking slowly and gracefully across the mud flats, then as Little Star's light flickered faster and faster, Brolga danced and danced and danced! The moon and stars looked down to see what all the commotion was about. Suddenly all of the stars in the universe started sparkling in time with Brolga's dance, and the whole sky was set alight in a joyful celebration. All the birds were amazed, they had never seen anything like it before. While the whole universe was dancing together, a remarkable thing happened. Brolga's wings had swept up the dust from the mud flats and it began to swirl around, reaching up towards the night sky. At the same time, the shimmer from the stars descended down towards the earth. Together the earth dust and the stardust formed a stairway to the heavens.

'Quickly,' said Brolga, 'here is your way home, Little Star. Climb up the stairway and dance along the shimmering light until you reach your place in the night sky.'

'Thank you,' said Little Star, but she was too weak to move. She had almost lost her final sparkle.

Brolga scooped Little Star up on her shoulders and ran towards the swirling stardust. She pulled out her largest flying feather and gave it to Little Star. Little Star, with her final spark, leapt up onto the stairway and Brolga's feather carried her into the heavens.

'Goodbye, Brolga!' she shouted as she

found her way home.

The other birds stood with their beaks gaping in awe.

'Can you teach us how to do that?' asked the birds.

'Of course,' said Brolga.

The very next night, all the birds gathered together with their finest feathers and all the stars greeted Brolga with their sparkles. Little Star was the brightest of them all.

'Everybody ready?' asked Brolga. 'Let's dance up a storm so all the fallen stars can find their way home.'

GECKO

&

BIG ROCK

Some children are just like the gecko in this story. They are brave and courageous and love sharing their discoveries. They are amazing children and inspire others to reach past the bounds of possibility.

Gecko loved exploring and finding new places. He was an adventurer, and had a great deal of knowledge about how the earth was put together. Whenever he returned from a journey, he insisted on telling all the animals about his travels. The animals grew tired of hearing Gecko's stories and told him he should spend more time at home instead of gallivanting around the countryside. But Big Rock loved Gecko's stories, and often sat with him on the top of the hill, gazing out across the land and wondering what lay beyond the horizon.

Gecko and Big Rock loved lazing in the sun during the day. At sunset, Big Rock glowed and sparkled from all the heat he had absorbed into the crystals surrounding his heart. Because of this, Gecko stayed close to Big Rock at night to keep warm.

One day a great cold descended across the earth. The sky turned grey and the sun seemed to completely disappear. Snow started to form across the earth and sky, and the rivers and oceans became still, trapping the water creatures beneath a blanket of ice. The birds and animals were very worried, they had never known anything like this before. It was too cold to venture outside, and even Gecko got frostbite on his toes trying to visit Big Rock.

Something had to be done. All the birds and animals got together for a meeting. The birds suggested flying through the clouds to make a path for the sun to shine through. So the next day, the strongest birds flew together in an arrow formation high into the sky. The clouds were so thick with frost and snow, the birds could not get through no matter how many times they tried. They fell back onto the frozen earth, exhausted and cold. Big Rock had been listening and watching the animals and wanted to help. He told everyone of a way to break through the clouds.

'If we get all the biggest and strongest rocks together, they can form a mountain high above the earth that will be able to pierce the clouds and find the sun,' said Big Rock.

'How are we going to find enough rocks to build a mountain?' asked the animals.

'I know where all the rocks are,' said Gecko. 'I have made friends with many of them on my travels. I'm sure they will help us,' he said.

'But it is far too cold for you to travel,' said the animals. 'How will you survive?'

All the animals offered warm fur and feathers to keep Gecko safe. The next day Gecko ventured out to find the biggest rocks across the landscape. However, after only a few days, Gecko had to return. He was almost frozen and needed to be nursed back to health before he could try again.

'I must go back out,' said Gecko.

'No,' said the animals. 'It is too dangerous. We will have to think of something else.'

But Gecko was very brave and determined to find the rocks. That night Gecko and Big Rock talked together about what they could do.

'I think I can help,' said Big Rock. ' I still have some heat left deep in the crystals around my heart that can keep you warm on your journey. I will take out some of the warm crystals and put them in a special pouch. If you keep it close to your heart, it will give you the strength you need to complete your journey.'

Gecko was very grateful to Big Rock and knew of the deep sacrifice Big Rock was making to help him and the others. Gecko tucked the pouch of warm crystals inside the fur kangaroo had given him to wear and set off to gather as many rocks as he could. All of the rocks were surprised to see Gecko arrive wrapped in fur but were very happy to help. They too had been worried but didn't know what to do.

Soon rocks from all over the land began

arriving and gathered at the top of the hill. All of the birds and animals worked together with the rocks to build the mountain. Big Rock was too ill to take his place with the other rocks. The deep scar created from giving Gecko the crystals had left him weak and brittle.

The mountain grew higher and higher, forging its way through the clouds. But when the final rock took its place, it was not quite tall enough to reach the sun on the other side. Something more had to be done. No one had ever climbed so high before, but Gecko summoned up all his courage and bravely made his way up the mountain to reach the very top.

Gecko stood as tall as he could on his

hind legs. He reached up through the clouds, stretching out his arm holding the pouch containing the warm crystals. When the crystals broke through the icy clouds, rain began to fall. The rain melted away the frost covering the earth. The grey clouds lost their colour and quickly disappeared as mist into the sky. The sunlight found its way through and warmed the earth. A beautiful rainbow settled over the landscape. All the animals cheered and the rocks rumbled in great relief and celebration.

Gecko scampered down the mountain as fast as his little legs could carry him. He knew he had to help his friend Big Rock. Big Rock was sitting by himself at the top of the hill. Big Rock was very cold and weak. Gecko gave Big Rock back the pouch, and the crystals were returned to their rightful place. It took some time, but eventually Big Rock got his strength back.

From then on, the mountain stood tall in the clouds, so the sun always had a pathway to the earth to warm the landscape. And Gecko continued on his adventures, returning to rest with Big Rock in the sun to regain his strength and share his stories.

PLATYPUS
&
RIVER

Some children are just like the platypus in this story. They have a thirst for knowledge, searching patiently for answers to solve the conundrums of life. They are incredible children and are always willing to share their knowledge.

When Platypus was a little platypup, he was always thinking about so many things that he felt muddled and couldn't get to sleep. River noticed him tossing and turning.

'Come and have a swim,' said River. 'Let the water calm your mind and help you to sleep.'

River was right. After a long swim, Platypus could think clearly and had the best sleep ever. Platypus would swim for hours studying all of the waterways. Platypus always told River what he had learnt on his journeys and River was fascinated by his great knowledge.

One day River was troubled and didn't know what to do. There was a stream that kept flowing the wrong way. Little Stream wouldn't follow the path that was drawn for him by the ancestors. This made the waterways muddy and salty and all the animals were complaining. Even the fish couldn't find their way anymore and kept bumping into each other.

'We can't drink from the waterholes anymore, River,' said the animals. 'What has happened to your beautiful water? We

will all die from thirst if Little Stream
keeps being naughty.'

'I am so sorry,' said River. 'I don't know
why Little Stream is so headstrong. I think
he wants to grow up too quickly and be a
big river instead of a little stream.'

'Well, if he doesn't behave soon, we
will have to build a dam and stop him
altogether,' said the animals, very upset.

'Oh, please don't do that,' River
pleaded. 'He will become a dry old river
bed if you stop him running. I will talk to
him and see what I can do.'

River tried talking to Little Stream, but
Little Stream wouldn't listen.

'You are just a big old boring river,' said
Little Stream rudely. 'I want to run to the

ocean and see the whales, then everyone will follow me instead.'

'But that is not the way it is meant to be,' said River. 'The land and the animals depend on us to bring them fresh water.'

Little Stream didn't care and turned away from River, forging a new path through the bushland.

Platypus was swimming along River when he heard the animals complaining. Because Platypus was so clever, he was the only one who could still navigate safely through the muddy waters. Platypus knew all the waterways and understood how the whole river system worked together to nurture the land and the animals.

A few days later when Platypus was

checking on some new water lilies, he
came across a black lake he had never seen
before. At the bottom of the lake slept
a beautiful serpent ancestor, the biggest
serpent of all time. He had slumbered
there for centuries after creating all of the
streams and rivers. But the lake was sick.
There was no fresh water coming into it
anymore and the water that was in the lake
was disappearing. Lake asked Platypus for
help.

'Platypus,' said Lake, 'can you find out
why none of the streams have come to
visit me? I am waiting for fresh water to
replenish the waterhole. I don't want to
disturb the serpent from his dreaming.'

'Of course,' said Platypus. 'I think I

know exactly what the problem is!'

Platypus went looking for Little Stream. He was hard to find as he kept changing course and disappearing. After much searching, finally Platypus found Little Stream trying to go up the side of a mountain.

'What are you doing?' said Platypus to Little Stream.

'Oh, not you as well. I am trying to find my own way,' said Little Stream. 'I want to be an important big river.'

'But you are important,' said Platypus. 'In fact you are one of the most important streams in our landscape.'

'I don't understand,' said Little Stream. 'I am just a trickle of water, I am not important to anyone.'

'Follow me and I will show you just how important you are,' said Platypus.

Platypus and Little Stream journeyed back across country together and along the way, Platypus explained to Little Stream how all of the waterways worked together, from the smallest trickle to the largest river.

'You are part of a very big family,' explained Platypus, 'and without you, we will all perish.'

'I had no idea. I thought I was all on my own,' said Little Stream.

When they arrived at Lake, Little Stream became scared.

'What is this place?' he asked, trying to

hide behind Platypus.

'It is the spirit lake of one of our serpent ancestors,' said Platypus. 'The lake is sick because the fresh water has stopped coming and the serpent will soon have to wake from his slumber to find out what is wrong. The serpent needs his sleep, as the earth needs his dreaming to survive. The lake can only be replenished by a stream of water small enough but strong enough to find its way through the rocks deep in the earth. None of the rivers can do this, so it needs to be a little stream who is very determined.'

'That sounds just like me!' said Little Stream.

'If you had followed the right path, you

would have found your way to the spirit lake,' said Platypus. 'Instead of seeing whales, you would have seen the largest and most beautiful ancestor serpent of all time. You can be headstrong, but you must also learn to listen and understand. You may only be a little stream, but you have the most precious water of all.'

Little Stream took a big breath and with all his might forged a path deep into the rocks, allowing the precious water to replenish the lake and the serpent to continue his slumber. Little Stream felt very proud.

'I would never have known what to do without you, Platypus,' said Little Stream.

All the animals and waterways rejoiced

and thanked Platypus for his patience and wisdom. Platypus often visited Little Stream and bathed in the spirit lake only they had seen.

FRILLNECK LIZARD
LIZARD
&
TREE

Some children are just like the frillneck lizard in this story. They have a natural ability to make us laugh and bring light relief to dark times. They are astounding children who can challenge us to see things differently and bring joy and colour into the world.

Frilly was a young frillneck lizard. Frilly was always mucking about and trying to entertain everyone. He loved to play jokes on his friends then run off into the trees laughing. Whenever anyone ran after him, they could never find him. He was very good at hiding and could stay hidden for a long time. The animals were all getting a bit fed up with Frilly.

'Silly Frilly. You never take anything

seriously, do you?' the animals chastised him.

'Sometimes you need to have a good laugh,' said Frilly, 'it can help you see things differently and bring back the colour in life.'

'Maybe, but you need to be more responsible,' the animals said grumpily.

One day Frilly was playing with a fire-stick, when all of a sudden there was a loud bang and Frilly was covered in smoke. When the smoke cleared, he realised he had burnt his lovely frill. He was so embarrassed he ran away under a big old gum tree to hide. Tree looked down at the little lizard whimpering under his branches.

'What is wrong?' asked Tree.

'I was being silly and burnt myself,' said Frilly.

'Let me see,' said Tree. Tree reached down and gently scooped Frilly up onto a big branch. He made a soothing balm with his eucalyptus oil and red-gum to help heal Frilly's wounds. Frilly was very grateful. From that time on, Tree and Frilly were great friends.

Frilly always went to Tree for help. Tree laughed at Frilly's silly pranks and loved watching him run for cover. Tree always gave him a place to hide and soothe his wounds. They would talk and tell stories for hours together.

Frilly was sitting in Tree one day

making up a new song when he noticed
the sky was turning grey.

'Must be a storm coming,' he said to
Tree.

There was no reply.

'Tree?' said Frilly. Tree look frightened
and his leaves were shaking. All of the
trees around him were trembling and the
rustling sound of the leaves grew louder
and louder.

'It's more than a storm,' said Tree.

The greyness quickly spread across the
landscape. This marked the beginning of a
very dark time for the earth. The landscape
was being destroyed and everyone was
frozen with fear. Frilly started showing the
animals how to hide away from the grey.

Tree was one of his greatest allies, as he was able to use his branches and leaves to cover the animals and stood tall to watch out for danger. He would rustle his leaves loudly to warn Frilly and the others when to hide and when it was safe. Frilly often snuck out at night to find food and check on everyone. He told funny stories to help the children settle and sang songs to the animals to keep up their hopes.

One morning, Tree rustled his leaves to let Frilly know it was alright to come out.

'The greyness is disappearing,' said Tree.

'So it is,' replied Frilly. Slowly all of the animals emerged from their hiding places to have a look around. The landscape was

not the same anymore. There were large
holes in the ground, many of the rocks
were broken and a lot of the trees had been
burnt. Even though the greyness had gone,
there was still a sadness over the land.
Frilly knew he had to do something. He
worked and worked, and then when he
was ready he invited all of the animals to
watch his new play.

Tree created a lovely green curtain
with his leaves and as he drew the curtain
back, Frilly appeared. The play showed
the animals how things used to be, as well
as everything they had been through. At
times everybody laughed and laughed,
at other times they shed many tears.
Everybody watched every moment. At

the end, there was loud applause and cheering. Never before had the animals understood just how important Frilly was. Frilly had never given up, but invented new ways to survive. He had looked after them in their darkest hour, kept them safe and comforted the little ones. But, most importantly, Frilly had lifted the sadness and brought back joy to the world.

Frilly had helped everyone to see things differently. He had helped the animals to come together with an open heart to share their grief and joy, and hope was restored.

The animals never chastised Frilly again but they did still get fed up sometimes with his jokes. Tree always stood watch just in case Frilly still needed a place to hide.

ABOUT THE AUTHOR

Helen Milroy is a descendant of the Palyku
people of the Pilbara region of Western Australia,
but was born and educated in Perth. Helen
has always had a passionate interest in health
and wellbeing, especially for children. Helen
studied medicine at the University of Western
Australia and specialised in child and adolescent
psychiatry. Helen is currently a Professor at
UWA, Consultant Child and Adolescent
Psychiatrist, and Commissioner with the
National Mental Health Commission. Helen was
recently appointed as the AFL's first Indigenous
Commissioner. This is her first book for children.

IF YOU LIKED THESE STORIES, YOU MIGHT LIKE:

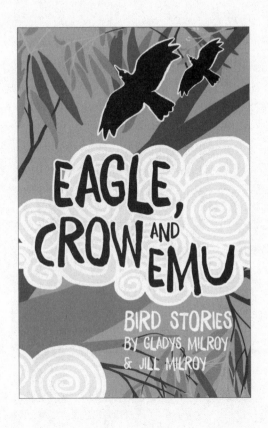

Birds who can't fly and snakes who
can; mistakes to be made and problems
to be solved; great enemies and even
greater friends — all this and more
in three exciting stories full of action,
adventure and birds!

Grandparents are special, and time spent with them is special, too. These four stories share some exciting, happy and even scary times exploring country in bush and beyond.

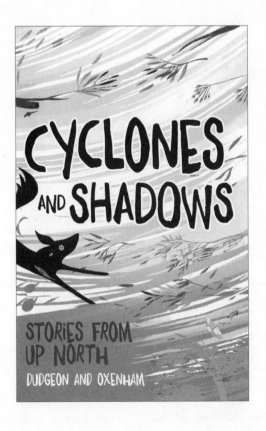

From an awesome sports car to
a terrifying cyclone, from magical
creatures to a haunted mango tree,
these four stories from up north are
full of adventure and excitement.

First published 2019 by
FREMANTLE PRESS
25 Quarry Street, Fremantle WA 6160
www.fremantlepress.com.au

Cover designed by Rebecca Mills.
Printed by McPherson's Printing, Victoria, Australia.

Wombat, Mudlark and other stories
ISBN: 9781925815818.

A catalogue record for this
book is available from the
National Library of Australia

Fremantle Press is supported by the State Government through
the Department of Local Government, Sport and Cultural Industries.

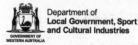